ALONE VOICE

The voice of unheard words

Presented by TAARE ZAMEEN PAR

FanatiXx Publication

AM/56, Basanti Colony, Rourkela 769012, Odisha

ISO 9001:2015 CERTIFIED

Website: www.fanatixx.in

"ALONE VOICE"

By: **Keerthi Somavarapu & Rahul Pasumarthy**

ISBN: 978-93-89557-17-6

POEM Book 1st Edition

Book Formatting: PHALGUNI JAGADEESH

Cover Design: RONAK

The opinions/contents expressed in this book are solely of the author and do not represent the opinions/ standings/ thoughts of FanatiXx

ACKNOWLEDGMENT

The completion of this anthology would not have been possible without the co -operation of all the co - authors.

This anthology is a hard work of the team where everyone has dedicated to each activity allowed to them and they have done the job fantastically.

Thank you Phalguni Jagadeesh for editing the book, with outmost dedication.

Thank you Taare Zameen Par and Gaurav Porwal for giving me the chance and helping me in every situation.

A big thanks to Fanatixx Publications, without your support this wouldn't have been possible.

Above all, thanks to Parents and God for their love and support.

Thank you every one for believing us!

Rahul Pasumarthy

(Compiler)

Presented by TAARE ZAMEEN PAR

ALONE VOICE

Born and brought up in Vizianagaram, Andhra Pradesh. He is a CA student apart from his studies; he wrote stories and motivational quotes, he is a moody writer and bookaholic. His dream is to inspire millions of people in following their dreams and motivate them to face their failure, believe and fall in love; he has wrote a lot about life, love, pain, healing and recovery.

Keerthi Somavarapu

(Compiler)

She is a person who is positive about every aspect of life, born & raised in Tenali, Andhra Pradesh. She completed her schooling and college in here; she is doing her masters at the moment. Apart from studies she loves to write poems and short stories, she always tries to put her feelings into words as she feels poetry is the beautiful ray of hope which guides her towards the new discoveries. This is her first anthology and she is looking forward to all that life gets for her.

INDEX

S.NO	Co-authors
31.	Pradeepti Sharma
32.	Prateek Jain
33.	Rajyalakshmi Donga
34	Rashmitha Kapuganti
35.	Riyanshi Gupta
36.	Saba Khan
37.	Shaikh Sohel
38.	Shailaja Rao
39.	Shipra Khanna
40.	Shrayan Raha
41.	Shrey Wadhawan
42.	S K Nandhini
43.	Sonal. Keshri
44.	Srimoyee Roy
45.	Suchismita Ghoshal
46.	Sumit Saha
47.	Sushil Kumar
48.	Swapnil Singh
49.	Tanya Gupta
50.	Vidushi Singh

FROM THE COMPILER'S DESK

Rahul Pasumarthy

@_blood_and_revolution

DARK TEARS

You are my first love of course first love is always the best one,

You are the person after my parents who started loving me without seeing me.

You are the first person whom I have seen when I opened my eyes even not my mother, I still remember that day you lifted me with your tiny hands and kissed me in my forehead.

It was the love at first sight moment for me;

We loved each other for almost 10 years but all suddenly you're left me and died alone.

Alone in the night with some feeling,
Sorry!

ALONE VOICE

With same feeling and a little sweat in my eyes and it looks like black in that dark, from that day I fell in love with the black because it holds all my emotions in it.

I never stop sweating from my eyes not to get out from the pain but to water your memories.

People called it tears,

But it was sweat due to suffocation of pain in the heart.

I have the only pill when I was low, and I called it as a pillow.

It wiped all my sweat when I was in low.

My bed become oceans with full of sweat in that boats of love are moving, which are carrying your memories.

As there is a continue flow of sweat I thought there will be no scarcity but now just like you those sweat to leave me.

People say that loneliness is position where you can love yourself, but you're taken me with you then whom to love.

SISTER LOVE

> I never thought that a few braided threads taught me what loneliness is?

Missing you on rakhi day justified it.

©Rahul pasumarthy

FROM COMPILERS DESK
Keerthi Somavarapu

@oneway_girll

❖ A voice, where I am all alone…

A voice, where I am lost totally…

A voice, where I am cheated completely…

A voice, where I am facing unfortunate fate…

A voice, Came to me,

Sounds, "You are alone, it's your strength and I am your strength".

❖ I light up my memories

Just to feel you again and again…

Because, I am all alone here without you where I lost my self in the dark.

Even you break my heart with your words I am here remembering you just

Like before when you call me as your love. I know you don't feel the same

Way, but I really can't get over you. It's better this way, A little loneliness

But better!!

CO-AUTHORS

Aarthi Sampath

-ROOTS HAVE SONGS

I survived everyday with painful sense of sounds piercing into my bones sharp as a dagger, I never thought words could kill, they labeled me worthless, I am a forgotten princess,

I was told I wouldn't survive as there were no cure, that I am broken soul they told I won't be fit to Love someone as the sleeping flowers don't bloom and with some strange distant voices telling me to quit this life,

I tried the chains of life, but it never broke free, because I am too scared to die, and with constant echoes of fate, nowhere yelling that I'll never be strong to follow my tribe of powerful women

But my beautiful mind never stopped loving this life, the solitude gave me space to breathe deep, telling that I deserve more to love myself than just being a wilted rose in bone Garden,

To help this vessel of self to rejoice the carnival of cosmos under the lilac skies and to imbibe in the psithurism of seasons to see myself evolve with hope

Holding reins of kindness and I know I'm love with roots that have songs

Singing symphonies of spring that I will live now, I am love, fluttering with bumblebee wings.

©Aarthisampath

Aashna Aga

-AGE IS JUST A NUMBER

Since the birth till now

We experience many things,

Pain is the part of our Life,

And at every age we pass through strife,

At some moments smile fade

Laughter disappear and we fall,

But still we try to shine,

Bothering about future

We get tense,

                                    Presented by TAARE ZAMEEN PAR

Thinking that we are wasting age,

But the thing is that,

At every age and stage

We must try, we must move,

Getting old every year is part of life,

So don't say that now you are old,

So don't say that now can't try for something new,

Look for things which make you happy,

Don't bother about the people,

Life Fong look for your age,

Life says, "it's just a number"...

-BELIEVE AND MOVE

When life force you to bow, you just be straight,

When life force you to hate, you just stick on love,

When life force you to give up, you just hold on,

When life force you to be weak, you pretend to be strong,

Be ALIVE and FOCUS on dream,

Just listen to your inner positive scream,

Keep on fighting with your troubles,

Till your strength get double,

Don't show it out, even if you are distress,

Under the burden of hope let negativity get press,

Don't block the path of IMAGINATION in your mind,

Accept OPPORTUNITY and continue to Struggle till the best you find,

When you do a MISTAKE, don't feel low,

TRUST yourself as the gloomy clouds of sadness will blow,

Have CONFIDENCE and let your thoughts shine more,

Keep on believing till the life open the SUCCESS door,

Your SMILE, you're trying you don't stop

Until you reach somewhere on top..

-DREAM TO FLY HIGH

Lift your soul,

To reach your goal,

Invigorate your spirit,

Probe the situation and learn from it...

Enamel your thoughts

And see what outcome you got,

ALONE VOICE

Try to survive from strafes,

Give s strong come back to your life...

Ages from past and present you refer,

Perceive its depth and see what it differ,

At any moment of life just don't lose hope,

As hopes are our shielding ropes....

Try to find hidden "You" within "You",

With the spark of success get flew

          Presented by TAARE ZAMEEN PAR

Abhishek Goyal

-ALONE BUT NOT ALONE

Down in crowded cities, everyone seems lonely,

living in overpriced flats with nothing homely,

an altogether new challenge for one & all,

with fight for every bit of space howsoever small,

stench of dirty politics, strangling everyone,

unemployment squeezing life out of young ones,

ALONE VOICE

No-one to give any warm embrace of comfort,

alone but not alone in this life of dire discomfort,
they talk here of good pleasant vibes and positivity,

but never they shy away to sow weeds of negativity,

every other person seems like cold hearted stones,

where are my old friends whom I used to bemoan.

Parents left behind to cope up by themselves,

their pain and grief becoming a part of myself,

praying constantly for my success and welfare,
working all day to pay for my fees and fares,
depression, lies, worries is all I am left with now
deadlines pinging me in place of my Tom's meows.

with no support except your own whatsoever,

posh life is just one of the biggest fat lie ever ,
amongst skyscrapers and metros there are lives,
where people live in congested slums like bee hives.
A long battle, life has become to be fought alone,

win it or it pings you to floor in its own harsh tone.

Everyone busy on their pagers and cell phones,
alone but not alone in this crowded mesh of bones,

                    Presented by TAARE ZAMEEN PAR

thick smoke layer together of lies and struggles
everywhere,
alone but not alone in world of forgotten morals here.

Aishwarya Asari

❖ Now every moment seems to be painfull

And its getting bitter and worsefull

If words and behavior gets changed

This heart doesn't know to change

For the amount of irritation it does inside

Even emotion plays its downsides

They say time will heal everything

But this clinging heart fails to understand anything

No matter what, bravery fights on edge

And this heart wants to break this bridge

Of pain and loneliness

❖ In a place of complete tranquility

Where words vanished by silence

Where sorrows evaporated by tears

Where joy passes with clouds

Where humbleness surrounds

Where question arises every now and then

Where rawness comes easily

Where right or wrong doesn't matter

And where mind meets with heart

❖ Dark nights

Moon light

Breezy air

Chilled weather

Cold drizzle

Warm clothes

Earthy fragrance N all I need is no one along with me.

Anasuya Singh Roy

-CONCRETE

Concrete I find outside and a jungle inside me too,

Plasters in my heart smoked up my mind with rue,

Cement within hardened my soul not to sing elegies,

Lone this spirit drinks wine of life in fuss human's grand dark parties.

Anjali Jha

Dear,

Lonely dreamer,

I know why you left your home. But don't worry for that. I know you are feeling alone but believe on me sometimes loneliness is the best companion to achieve your dream and it will help you in the worst phase too. Sometimes when the world is too busy in themselves and you try to talk or to share something and in that condition when you won't get someone then it will give a worst feeling and it can give a diverse effect on your mind and body. But when you live alone then you can think only for yourself because self love and self respect is a great thing for anyone which gives immense pleasure in yourself. Life become intoxicating if someone present around you but they are not your best companion. But when you are a lonely dreamer then you can do everything with yourself without taking help of anyone present around you. Sometimes to give peace and happiness to yourself, loneliness is must. But loneliness is a word which gives only negative impact on someone's mind that you are in stress and suffering from disease,

so you always try to live alone but it is wrong concept. Just think about old era when saint sat in the forest or mountain for penance for several years ago and they did not that they were suffering from stress but only due to the reason to give peace and happiness to their inner soul.

Yours,

Well Wisher

Anjali Kaushik

-I WOKE

I woke up
And saw nothing around,
I woke up
And there wasn't any sound.

I remember
Everything was dark & damp,
I remember
I reached out for the lamp.

Each bit
Seemed lifeless and still,
Each bit
Had a vacancy to fill.

I realised
I was there alone
I realised
Everything was out of zone.

I stood up
And opened the windows
I stood up
To get a glimpse of sunlit meadows.

I let
The light seep in,
I let
The darkness vanish from within.

-THE DARKNESS OF NIGHT

This night
This cold breeze,
This shivering
But sitting with ease.

This moon
These stars,

These thoughts
About the scars.

Those days
Those moments,
That rage
And those amusements.

Those
Made me stronger,
Upon those thoughts,
I ponder.

-I WISH!

I wish, I had a lamp
Which was always lit,
Lighting-up every bit.

I wish, There was
A path never-ending,
And which lead to nothing.

I wish, There was
Just happiness all around,
And to nothing it was bound.

I wish to watch

 Presented by TAARE ZAMEEN PAR

ALONE VOICE

The stary sky all night,
With the stars shining bright.

I wish to land
In unknown meadows,
And watching how nature grows.

I wish to be lost,

In my own world.

     Presented by TAARE ZAMEEN PAR

Anjana Agarwal

-NOT STOPPING TEARS

When I see sun with my Naked eye...

A tear rolls down,You know why...

Because sun is so far That I can't touch

You can feel its warm But u can't touch...

In same way when you are

In love you feel warm

But when you are hurt

And when you see picture With your naked eyes

A tear rolls down...

Presented by TAARE ZAMEEN PAR

-MY DREAMS

When I dream I see I am a queen
But when I get up I see I am a house wife...
When I dream I see I am a magical Women
But when I get up I see I am a normal human being
When I dream I see I can fly
But when I get up I see I am in land..
This is the fact which I realize when I am awake is truth and
when I sleep its fake... be in real life not Dream...

-GOOD FOR NOTHING

Once I got to hear that you are good for nothing
I thought if I am good for nothing
Then how come I came so far
In my life,
I realise I am the person who Is good for everything
That is why someone said
You are good for nothing
Its because the things which
I can do no one else can do
From that day I say I am the best..

          Presented by TAARE ZAMEEN PAR

Anmol Singh Mehta

❖ Kabhi Kabhi hum kisi insan ko itna apna maan lete hai ki uske Door Jane Se humari Rooh tak hil jati hai kyunki woh sayad hume pyar karta ho ya nhi lekin humara pyaar ek dum sacha hota hai

Teri yaad aaii to thoda udaas ho jaoonga

Zindagi se phir ek baar niraash ho jaoonga

Kabhi socha bhee na tha aisa bhee hoga

Teri khushi ke liye mai khud ko rulaoonga

Arko Chakraborty

-CRAZY FRIENDS

The priceless prize I got...

The artless art I got...

The senseless thought I got...

The heartless heart I got...

The scented blossom I got...

The sollitary soul I got...

The naughtiest fuel I got...

And the craziest friends I got...

Banasmita Behera

-SOLITUDE

I am never alone
My dreams are with me,
My aspirations and their expections
I love to toil for their realisation .
To put me and them on top
Because the world demands ,
Nothing but the best.

I am never alone
Your thoughts are with me
Those keep my spirit elated,
Your memories never fade

ALONE VOICE

Through this desertion in disguise of crowd
You never make me feel out.

I am never alone ,
My parents' support is with me
It makes me feel stronger everywhere
With this courage, everything I can do.
It gives me spirit of go, get it
Except infinity for sky is the limit.

Presented by TAARE ZAMEEN PAR

Bhavya M Jain S

❖ Makes some noise,

As you have a wonderful voice.

Celebrate life,

It's the best choice.

❖ Everyone has a voice,

We must make a choice.

We don't know if it may sound nice,

But we must raise our voice to Raise ourself.

ALONE VOICE

❖ **L**-Low

O-out of order

N-nasty

E-effected by taunts of the society

L-lead to

I-incorrect

N- negative moves &

E-envyied by others success

S-screaming at thyself & waiting for thy

S-streaming time to come.

Bindiya Amethiya

-ONCE AGAIN

Unknown desires chasing me!
Making path anyhow
Reached
Knocked
Triggered my senses
I am witnessing
Me, myself thinking
To open the door or not?

-BEFORE I LEAVE HOME

Let me breath once again

                    Presented by TAARE ZAMEEN PAR

Let me embrace once again
Let me desire once again
Let me hug once again
Let me merge once again
To the shadows of our eternal moments hidden through
last night

-THE CITY SLEEPS

Neither mind agrees
Nor heart want to
Waiting..Waiting..
Endless waiting for you
The smell you left in my soul that night makes me
longing for you more deep

ALONE VOICE

Burhanuddin Shayar

-TRY, CRY AND DIE

Yes I am trying
But from inside
I am dying
I can't that feeling
I always hide
Like feelings died

I don't want to win
But I am trying to win
That situation and my agitation
I can't explain in words
Pain that I can't gird

Really don't want to try but trying
Looks I dont want to die but dying

        Presented by TAARE ZAMEEN PAR

Trying crying denying and doing
And yes i dont want but I am winning
But in this, special one I am loosing race
I will win but someone I am loosing

-MEMORIES

Those early morning walks
Every day and night we used to talk
Missing those days those walks and talks
You are my heartbeat and ticking clock.

You are the only clock ticking in my heart
You are far away from me but also my heart dart
You are not missing i feel your presence my sweet
heart
Your memories your thought are always in my heart

No matter how far you are
You are in my mind and in my heart
My heart beat beats with your memories
Your memories with me is treasury of my heart

Dhivya Aynan

-"DO YOU KNOW WHAT'S THE TIME NOW?"

Sandhiya heard her mom's voice from the kitchen and realized that she would be missing her college bus today. Priya, Sandhiya's sister grabbed her lunch box and was in a hurry to catch her school van. It was a small, but an ecstatic family.

She has got everything in her life. An affectionate mom, a compassionate dad and an amazing sister. Life was very easy for her. Everyone whom she met were being so sweet to her.

She felt nervous all of a sudden as her dad hasn't returned from office yet. It was already 7:15 am and something was disturbing her mind. Why hasn't her dad arrived yet?

A loud ring of the phone disrupted her thoughts and she was about to pick the call.

"You didn't have your breakfast yet, remember ?"

This was the nth time that mom has been shouting. She picked up the call. All she could hear was a loud siren.

"Is this Mr.Baskar's home ?"

A shaky male voice asked her. What she heard further had broke her heart into pieces. Seeing her mom in tears, she could sense that something disastrous had happened. She didn't speak a word and left in a hurry. Both of the sisters stood froze and were unable to predict what was really happening.

The loud siren of the ambulance almost made them dizzy. All they could see was that their dad was put in an electric ice box. What a plight is this? The voice that she heard yesterday won't be able to speak again. Who would console her when she cries? She wanted to kill her eyes when she saw her dad turning into ashes.

This nagging pain was unbearable. He left Sandhiya, Priya, and his beloved wife all alone. Loneliness and desertion was already killing them. Sandhiya didn't want this situation to persist and wanted to put a smile on her mom's face again. She couldn't see her sister crying. She wanted to raise up again.

She wanted to become as an IAS officer. Her sister motivated her and her mom gave all the support that she needs. She knew that it's not going to be easy, but she didn't give up. She studied day and night.

Every time when she felt tired, she thought of her dad and studied even more.

Yes, she is an IAS officer today.

Loneliness and desertion is like a ball. The more you hit, the high you rise.

Turn your pain into power.

Drishti Sapru

❖ There was something about your presence,

The one that made me forget my existence,

Oh! How lonely I was upon you going away,

Looking for answers in you,

But the picture changed,

Knew I couldn't accept change,

But wish someone had told me,

That looking for myself was the only answer I needed,

That solitude was the only solution to everything that happened.

Harika U V

-LONELINESS

Tells you about yourself

Fills you with sadness

BUT...

If you try...

You can change that sadness into
ENCOURAGEMENT

-LONELINESS

A power that helps you find what you are

-LONELINESS

A feel that is developed in our heart

When we feel that no one is beside us.

Ishani Agarwal

-SECOND CHANCE

When life gives me..

A second chance..

To pick up my life from where it had fallen,

I take it.

When life gives me

An opportunity..

To correct my mistakes..

I take it.

When life gives me

Happiness again and again..

And even though I know

It may be shortlived again..

I still take it..

-I HAVE WAITED FOR..

You to feel the way I feel for you..

I have waited for you to understand me..

I have waited for you to love me like i do..

Its been soo long..

But all I do is wait..

And you are too selfish..

Here, I keep waiting for you..

And there, you are busy with someone else too..

They say love is a nasty thing..

Now I believe it to be true !!

-WHEN A LOVED ONE LEAVES..

You are filled with a void..

But at times,

Letting that person go..

Is better than holding on to something..

Something.. that was broken a long while back..

Something.. that eases the ache in your heart..

Something.. that ends a dragged relationship..

At times, someone comes to fill that void..

And at times, you have to fight alone !

Ishika Agarwal

-SADNESS

Sadness creeps in like

A creeper

Slowly and steadily

But consumes everything inside you

Sadness creeps in like

A thief

It comes quietly

And steals your happiness.

-LIFE IS DIFFERENT

Life is too short

To entertain useless people .

To be boring .

To get ignored or ignore people .

To put my nose in other person's business.

To get hurt or

To get angry.

But

It is too long

To be fun .

To be joyful .

To be adventurous.

To be honest and fair.

And to be a lovely person .

Kaustubh Vats

❖ Loneliness is my only friend

I can feel her every time

And I am enjoying her company

Our relationship will never end

I usually cry in her lap

I can share anything with her

She will never let me go

She usually wraps me in her hands

ALONE VOICE

Whenever I count the stars

Whenever I scribble with my pen

Whenever I feel scared

I found her holding my hand

There is no replacement of her

She is the best

She always appreciate me

And motives me to do my best

She is better than this fake world

She is better than a fake friend

She will never cheat on me

So she is my best friend.

Khushi Garg

-FORLORN

The space in the center of my chest has been void since you left,

It feels like I am floundering with no destination to achieve,

I call out for help but the space around me is suffused with a deafening silence,

I try to put my pieces back together and end up scattering them beyond my reach,

The darkness has become my best friend,

The empty walls have become my only support,

ALONE VOICE

My tear stains have painted the pillow covers in an unnamed hue,

And I, I am breathing, just breathing.

I search for you everywhere, in all the crowds and gatherings,

But the only place I find you is in my mind and memories,

The food on my table is left untouched,

"Your" side of the bed left undisturbed,

My ears are yearning to hear your voice,

But I guess I don't have that choice,

You said that you would wait for me,

And yet, here I am, waiting for thee,

The words you left unsaid are waking me up late at night,

The love you gave still feels so bright.

The demons in my head are hunting me down,

My withering self is drowning deeper and deeper,

My soul is scathed and my thoughts are loud,

ALONE VOICE

And I am woken only by my nightmares,

The deepest scars are the hardest to heal,

The friendless lanes the hardest to walk,

Now all I want is for this silence to cease,

And for the death to wrap it's cold arms around me.

Mahalakshmi

❖ A lonely bench in a park

Alone me and my dairy

Reading stories of life

Happened long ago

Tears fell down reading

A sad beginning of marriage life

Peaceful after girl child

Time spent alone crying

Those days like hell

Fed up of being alive

ALONE VOICE

Fed up of loneliness

Learnt to live independent

Learnt life lessons

Learnt how to be confident

Learnt how to self motivate

Lead life alone bravely

Happy life loneliness teaches.

Mahmoda Sultana

-DEPRESSION

Why do I feel pain, I don't know the reason,

Suddenly I do cry like rain shed in the winter season.

But again I can't cry though I feel my scars attacking like acid,

Even I became wordless and my sore can't bleed.

Sometimes sleepless lonely nights are there,

Sometimes I lie on the bed and what people do say I don't care.

During daytime I do close the door,

And even I don't want to give a single step on my green moor.

I started hating the notion of brightness,

While once I used to afraid of darkness.

Often I cancel my plans and creating my own cafe, I know.

But a black shadow is always there who forbade me to go.

I want to cry, yell or raise my high voice-

But in the end keeping my mouth shut is my only choice.

Loneliness poisoned me to sit in the corner of my dark room,

It made me believe that my both days and nights are gloom.

Here, I am fighting with myself life became a war-

Where, I just want to cross the spiritual bar.

Yes, I want to die and I am not afraid of dying,

But I am afraid of losing.

I am alive, but dead inside leading a zombie's life,

ALONE VOICE

Where, I am smiling knowing that something is stabbing my back with sharp knife.

My own thoughts are my own rebels,

Every time which screams harder like a devil in the hell?

I became the murderer of my own happy face,

My mind is the scariest place.

I know it's nothing but depression, which changed everyone's life perception!

Manisha Goyal (Musona)

❖ Loneliness is a connecting LINE for future.

Lone ---- LINE ---- Ss

Lone ----Lost & Negative thoughts are fighting with positive to draw a

LINE of

Ss- Silence in mind and Strength in body to create better future.

❖ Being lonely and Single

ALONE VOICE

Does not mean,

SAD & UNHAPPY

For me, Loneliness is My Best Friend Forever

Because, Loneliness

L - Loves me like my parents

O- Observe my moves like my best advisor

N- Nicely handle my emotional trauma like a best buddy

E- Emotionally supports me like a best partner

L- Lifts me up

I- Ignores my angry mood.

N- Not only ignore my angry mood, but also helps me

E- Ending the trauma of depression &

S- Sad phase of my life and make me feel like a

S- Shining light in the crowd.

ALONE means...

A - Allow me sometime, to

L- Lighten

O- Or to

N - Nicely balance the

E - Emotional trauma running in my mind.

Monika Srijana Ram

❖ I wish my pillow could speak,

It would tell you about all the things that I never spoke about,

All the tears I shredded,

My untold stories,

How every night,

I used to linger to the end of the bed in between fighting and letting go,

Thinking what my father told,

I'm his beta and I can keep up even with my foes,

I'm strong and brave, and I don't necessarily have to let go,

I understood everything then,

But now dad,

With you gone,

I'm all alone,

Nobody else to talk or to hone,

I have became this monster,

I can't face this mirror anymore,

Daddy I'm afraid of myself,

I can't survive without you no more.

I need you today and forever,

Mend me into something you would want me to be,

I love you Daddy,

I want to live with you,

Just let me be.

- Your lost daughter

❖ And here the night has fallen,

ALONE VOICE

But my tears didn't,

Stars has came,

But the hope didn't,

Moon has came,

But peace didn't,

Light has faded,

But my pain didn't.

Clouds has darkened,

But my soul didn't.

The time stood still,

Leaving the memories behind,

I walked away.

I had written millions of memories and dreams,

Embroided them in the constellation of stars,

Naming them as escapade,

Which is to remind you?

That, I still exist.

After the tragic storm,

You have forgotten me,

But even when millions of distance apart,

ALONE VOICE

You are still very close to my heart.

I cry very much every night that the pillow gets soaked with my tears,

Each night I feel I'm falling apart from myself,

I'm losing my happiness,

I wonder if the stars from those constellations can grant me a wish,

I would then wish to go back in time and wish you,

Yes, you are my only wish darling.

I lied and left and that's only the mistake I want to undo,

But, it's too late,

My letters cannot reach you.

You are on the other side,

But at least you are happy,

And this is what gives me hope everyday to wake up,

I still dream about you coming back to me though,

I love you today and I will love you till my last breath.

-Your babe

ALONE VOICE

❖ You had changed your way,

You closed the door,

I have seen through the broken window,

When I took the tour of your memory lane,

You reddened our door,

Back then it was for love,

But now it showed hate.

I opened the gate and took a step further,

You know what I found?

The guilt and the blame.

I thought I was your love,

But it turns out I was only your game.

The game you played very well,

You made me fell in love with you,

But you have no idea what it cost you,

Unknowingly by trying to win, you had lost too,

I can see in your eyes, the guilt & blame was there because

After somehow you got a pinch of feelings for me,

Even though I was your game,

You knew I was something more,

This is why you were afraid to have me,

And you threw me then.

And on that day,

"Honey, with me you have lost yourself too".

Nandini Kulkarni

❖ I gave my all

You think how it is when you actually give your all to someone

Well,

It's the feeling when you take out your time for them

It's the feeling when you wait for them in the night even when you want to sleep

It's the feeling when you wish that they feel for you as much as you do

But apparently Love's not a easy one to conquer after all

They, at last leave you the moment they find someone better

And you, my dear, you just sit and realize it's not goanna be same

 And accept that they won't give you their all

❖ Is To Was

His voice trembled with outrage

Looking at her

He pushed her far from his arms

Wishing for her absence

His wish became reality

The moment he knew that

Her presence turned

From is to was

❖ Oh what a broken heart faces ,

Those cried out nights,

Those scars on the wrists,

Those heart burns.

                    Presented by TAARE ZAMEEN PAR

But the most feared,

The loneliness.

Narmatha Thukkaivel

❖ She is in a feast

Provided with flavorsome dishes

She resolves to eat least

And wishes

To pack those to her grandchildren

She looks at the knishes

Hot tears fill in

The reality flashes

Dishes of ampleness

Are vanishing in the gloam

As she is in loneliness in an old age home.

Parul Singh

❖ It was tough for me to walk beside you or match your footsteps. I really wanted to hold your hands while covering those sandy beaches. But I would fall short of breath every time I tried catching up with your pace.

  You know, a lot of times, I would stop in between our walks, just to watch you   turning into a blurry image. It was kind of healing to watch you walk from behind, leaving your footprints...

Ah, and you never believed in turning back.

I always complained how much I miss holding your hands but you never allowed me to do so.

Well, holding onto something was never your thing. Everyone around you took it otherwise; but that's who you were.

And that's who I loved.

You were so unlike me.

You were all about strong winds, wildflowers, abandoned buildings, and oceans. I, on the other hand, was more into sand houses, paintings, slow music, and cubicles. I loved staying in boundaries, not crossing the lines.

For you, it was so hard to return to the same place and watching the same set of faces. Had it been upon you, then you might have never returned to yourself too!

You never permitted me to capture you in anything - either in my heart or my poetries.

And I tried - I tried very hard - to not search for the stories inside you. But I failed drastically.

I remember that morning when you took a promise that I wouldn't be sad and cry for more than four days if ever you left. Well, I knew that you were going to leave. Sooner.

I knew that you loved yourself but disliked equally. Being in your own company, staying in your own skin was too much for you.

I promised you.

And just like any other day, your image started diminishing into nothing.

The people around me think that they can capture you into this wooden box but hey, they're wrong. Your frame can be captured but not your soul. I know you are happy... The flowers around me are in a jolly mood. They are screaming your name. You are a part of their family now.

Me?

I am happy too. I have lived my eternity with you. I am at peace and yeah, smiling too.

Presented by TAARE ZAMEEN PAR

Phalguni Jagadeesh

-LET ME FLY

Let me fly,
To reach the sky.

Don't cut my wing,
One is already sling.
Let me fly,
Till I reach high.
I have dreams,
Which are still in reams?
A lot I cried,
Now my tears are dried.

                    Presented by TAARE ZAMEEN PAR

ALONE VOICE

Let me fly,
To reach the sky.

I bleed blue,
Trying to create a hue.
Don't cuss,
Life is already a mess.
Don't break my hope,
I just have an option of rope.
Let me live,
There's nothing more I can give.

Let me fly,
To reach the sky.

Help me if you can,
One's life is of short span.
Show some mercy,
Have a little courtesy.
Be the kind,
One could rarely find.
Take a stand,
Be a helping hand.

Let me fly,
To reach the sky.

Pooja Trivedi Raval

❖ I am used to be alone
In the group of people in market
I am used to be alone
With the buried feelings to let

I am used to be alone
With someone whom I love the most
I am used to be alone
Where I was habituated to be lost

I am used to be alone
In my entire life

Presented by TAARE ZAMEEN PAR

I am used to be alone
Doesn't matter as a mother or a wife

I am used to be alone
When I am looking for someone
I am used to be alone
With the support of none

This journey taught me to be mine
In any situation to be fine
Do not expect from anyone
As I am used to be alone...

-A LETTER TO MY LONELINESS

My dear loneliness,

How are you? Have you listed the names of the near and dears who had left you in me?

It is an awesome experience to be with you. I came to know that how difficult I am to be loved. Do you know it was too difficult to be with you when I was pretending to be in some function? Have you remembered our first meet? On the occasion of the marriage at some near one's place?

I was afraid of you on that day. Because I did not know that you would be my best companion of my life. I felt myself helpless when in laws and husband had chosen to leave for their group and I was new in the family. I literally tried to find someone to talk and be with. Fortunately I didn't find anyone.. And I met you...

I just had written you a letter that you are now a part of mine... No one can separate us. I wanted to thank you for everything I learnt from you. I really appreciate your support to help me not to lose my trust from the feelings. Even you had helped me to know my feeling with more better explanation and much better understanding...

I only have a complain that why you don't be only mine... The other people will not appreciate you like me. Please be mine forever and leave others with their joy and happiness

Yours only,

SMIT Pooja Raval.

❖ To my dear loneliness

ALONE VOICE

The excitement is never less

I have good news
It might be like different views...

It is the only news after I met you
I tried however not able to let you

Now we become a family
With two children in the family
Sadness and tears are
New member of our family...

Now this family looks like complete
I am enjoying having the growth of it

Nothing is a bit less
But the way it impress

I heartily thank you
To be with me when no one was there
Friends like you
People can find rare...

Pradeepti Sharma

-A QUAINT SOLITUDE

Rings in the time of celebration and revelry,

And the city dances to the festive tunes,

A souk in the old city decks up to enthrall the shopaholics,

Who throng its stone paved streets filled with hues of glee and gaiety,

Exuberance fills the tranquil cool air of the souk from dawn till midnight,

ALONE VOICE

And the balmy winter noon now shined in all its pomp and glory over each and every niche of the old city,

Amongst this crowded existence, resided a lonely soul,

A tad little boy, in his early teens, played a balsam flute,

His tattered clothes and sole less feet revealed his humble existence.

To earn his daily bread he sat on the dusty street and pumped his tiny heart whole day,

His melodies strummed the strings of time with reflections of life's bleak reality,

Some passersby dropped a penny or two in his crooked copper bowl,

While some just didn't acknowledge his voice in the market noise,

Still he continued to play his soul's thoughts with deep devotion,

I wondered such is the reality of life, sharing the same space and time, some relish all luxuries and some just manage to get a meager morsel,

Still my heart rejoiced that despite being privileged, we continue to live in utter loneliness, and what this boy was blessed with was a quaint solitude.

Prateek Jain

-THE DOPE OF LONELINESS

Whether it's dazzles of day,

Or night of darkness,

I am always high,

On dope of loneliness,

The clutter of outdoors,

Bring music to ears,

The silence of indoors,

Make eardrums tear,

                    Presented by TAARE ZAMEEN PAR

ALONE VOICE

Company disappoints,

With mundane triviality,

Self obsessively I explore,

Music, books, art & rationality,

Some call me hysterical,

Because of jealousy,

Some even think mystical,

Due to naivety,

They can never realize,

Joy of one's own company,

While busy to monetize,

Wonders of humanity.

Rajya lakshmi Donga

❖ Loneliness is better than losing our self-respect.....

Loneliness is better than rejected by everyone....

Loneliness is better than feeling alone among our loved ones....

Loneliness is better than knowing hatred....

Loneliness is better than being cheated....

Loneliness is better than feeling disappointed.....

Loneliness is better than heart break...

Loneliness is the time to enjoy our self-company....

Loneliness is better to focus on our abilities....

ALONE VOICE

Loneliness is better to know ourselves...

It's the way we can develop our self what we want to be if we realize........

Rashmitha Kapuganti

-HELLO, MY LONELINESS,

I am Mayuri, when I am at the age of 10yrs Mom, and dad left me in the hostel in that age, I am much pampered to my parents. When i entered into the hostel I don't know how to talk with others because my place is a village. Here all use to talk in English. Suddenly, my life became like a parrot in a cage without freedom. My shadow became my friend no one will be there forever, but my shadow is there with me up to my last breath. I use to share all my feelings with my heart. I can't express my feelings out with anyone. Everyday my hunger filled in a dustbin. Every night cried alone.

Nevertheless, no one cares me. My Nights gone with cry and thoughts. Why my parents not understanding my feelings? I went to the sleep with bag full of tears. Every pain has a wonderful gain. One day my friend Tapaswini came to me asked what happened. Why you are looking sad? I replied that I am fine. She gave chance to share feelings. Then I shared my emotions with her. She told do question itself then you can come out with your happy life. Why you came for? What's your goal? What are you looking for?

End of the day, I recollected all questions But I didn't get one answer because up to now I am dumb. I have to show my Talent. I got confidence after her motivation. Without her I won't be best in this world. She gave me a confidence to live strong. I came out of loneliness by reading all inspirational novels.

 I developed my language by reading all books. I covered my loneliness with write ups. Then I published in books. Now I became a best writer. I am very thanking full to Tapaswini.

Yours,

Mayuri.

Riyanshi Gupta

❖ After a breakup, there is a great feeling of loneliness that overcomes us. For so long, we felt that we were a part of something bigger than ourselves. Suddenly we are left with the realization that we no longer have another to lean on. The loneliness is overwhelming. We have become used to having someone with us all the time. We probably made all our decisions together. To suddenly be alone after intense togetherness is a very lonely feeling.

    Presented by TAARE ZAMEEN PAR

Saba Khan

❖ In loneliness, we feel that there is no one to care,
love…
But it is not so,
It is just our thinking.
We feel alone in crowd,
And if we want, we can find love for ourselves even
in loneliness

Shaikh Sohel

❖ Walking in a street

Alone with the shattered feelings

Deep down as I entered

It's all about loneliness with a broken heart...

❖ Being single is not a matter of loneliness

It's what being independent and accepting the responsibility towards nation.

❖ **Heart says: -** living alone is like living in a prison..

But,

Mind says: - living alone is better than living in a heard of betrayal ones..

Shailaja Rao

-THE SEA OF LIFE

Sea died amidst the dark of the storm,

A volatile vortex spun and was done,

The mighty ship hit an iceberg and lost its firm,

The wood splintered, it cracked and poked out under the eclipsed sun,

The ship's wreckage touched oblivion, a dilapidated sum,

The dark azure encroached as the sky fuelled to burn.

No soul apart from me here,

ALONE VOICE

Only a flamingo in the run, who swore to dare,

To give me company as the sky is our only stare,

Loneliness crept in smooth and clear,

Our languages collided to be turned to dust with no care,

We kept counting the stars in pair,

A bond blossomed as we pulled near,

I believed if doom was near but it was still fair.

This journey across the coast,

It's long and tardy that roast,

No passenger gives company forever moreover they boast,

Every soul is their ghost.

❖ Love is a need,

Not a luxury,

Like water is a need,

As the lands dry without it hastily,

Loneliness fathom breed,

As love entwines passionately.

Shipra Khanna

❖ Occupied I am

By loneliness

T's has been my friend

For a long time

It's not strange for me

It's in me and I am in it

I enjoy myself

In my loneliness
Never do I feel

Presented by TAARE ZAMEEN PAR

ALONE VOICE

It's bounded me Feel relaxed

In presence of my loneliness.

❖ O! my love

You yes you

Have given me

This loneliness

Am going to die

For I love you

You are my life

This loneliness

Irritates me

It's my enemy

Come soon

For I am going to

Die of this loneliness

❖ At its best loneliness

When feeling low it becomes friend

When studying it becomes compulsory

While partying never comes near.

Shrayan Raha

❖ It's not about the chances I gave.

It's about the efforts you didn't made,

& the trust you lost from me day by day.

❖ No longer can I receive her messages.

No longer can my fingers scroll her name.

But deep inside, my heart always carries a hope.

❖ While I was totally consumed by love, I broke.

Now I need more love to heal my wounds.

Maybe it's true "What heals us also break us."

Shrey Wadhawan

❖ Take that "Pain" out from my Heart.

Please shut the door of thoughts & emotions.

Leave my "loneliness" unbroken.

Stop being, judgmental for a while.

Let me cry & break this depression.

❖ Loneliness is real with full of emotions & self-company.

It may freeze like Ice & bust like lava.

Emptiness becomes close allies and time turns into biggest enemy.

Treat & welcome with care & affection.

❖ Not the end yet. There is still a lot to understand.

Let alone deal with terrifying reality.

There is also this sudden feeling of emptiness & loneliness.

I coped with living in a bubble, dealings with my loneliness & hoping everything would be okay.

S K Nandini

❖ Loneliness is word ,but it push a person into depression and

It kills them....

We have friends to ease our loneliness,

Leaving friends push into loneliness,

Breakup left us in a lonely path,

Fighting with siblings is also a kind of loneliness,

Everyone needs each other companies,

We become lonely when there is no one to share our feelings,

Everyone face a kind of loneliness in part of life,

We should overcome our loneliness and we have to divert our mind to

Concentrate on something else, so that we may able to

Forget our loneliness.

Sonal Keshri

❖ The kindest hearted people are those who listen to each and every problem from someone's past, get worried, they see their best future friend in them and completely manage to ruin their present themselves.

❖ Success is not something served to you; rather you need to work on every ingredient for a perfect recipe.

❖ Dear you Where ever you are lonely,

ALONE VOICE

Take your time but do come one day

Make a forever stay.

Srimoyee Roy

-"THE LEFT OUT ONE"

Last meeting was then when the sun was above us,

Since then I am a fragile figure.

Before the stars could again bind us together,

We drew miles apart for the sake of forever.

Miles were so hard to count, that the hearts crashed without any duly tune.

Thoughts were immensely difficult, resulting in explosive decisions.

Which burnt the innocence prevailing in me?

ALONE VOICE

Your promises confused me,

Your expressions fooled me.

I hope you be the happiest moving away from me,

And so I am trying to be...

You are the distorted chapter of my life,

Grieving and howling for the moment I fell for you.

I regret my emotions to build a home in your vicious world.

I was encapsulated with the loneliness,

Waiting for a hand to recover me...

Alas I was foolish.

This will be the last verses before its dawn..

Everything is "Blackened ".

The bright day failed to write our fortune together,

 What can a dark night recite for us?

-"BEYOND"

 I believed in you, to be my protagonist,

But, you were proved an antagonist!

Every time I looked at you, I thought you were a synonym of my life.

Yet again, you were the antonym.

Phrases and clauses always defined you in my book of grammar.

But, I blurred with the real vision.

Pretences and hopes welled me up with expectations,

But, wait were you even present in that situation?

I was busy weaving a home for us,

Little was I aware that you were only the one,

Replacing bricks of glee, with flaws.

The hollowness still bewilders me inside,

I walked the lane of sullenness muting my grief,

Holding hands with vividness,

To an unknown place with extreme suddenness.

  Presented by TAARE ZAMEEN PAR

Suchismita Ghoshal

-DESPONDENCY

The dark room beckons me, filled with an icy street of frozen blood.

Sunset bids & the night laughs, I procrastinate on going further.

My chained feet & squeezed mind, Pluck some motionless memories.

 Silent screams ocean deep, Tears turn into vapors;

I visualize my drooped face, in the mirror of my caged soul.

ALONE VOICE

Forbidden alley of their company, Scratches roughly on my delicate heart.

I found no way of surviving, for the plastic outlets of my skin

Lost the battle of emotions, I witness my nerves shrieked in agony,

Tranquility envelopes my heart, I sip the wine of loneliness.

Calamitous & troublesome;

Thoughts of my peculiar mind, Narrowed the tricky gaps of hopes.

Crowded with some fiery laughs,

I still hide my blood-patched heart, Sculptured by some blind trust & betrayals.

I don't repent on being alone, I cry for my softness & tenderness.

I don't yarn for another masked stranger; I crave for a strong heart.

Storms inside my pulsating blood vessels calm down with the passing nights.

Morning smokes the new warmth, Assurance comes & goes.

ALONE VOICE

I touch a tender leaf to feel the truth,

The truth of isolated dreams, the truth of a journey of new life.

Will it be my company in solitude?

I repeatedly query it, & the answer is still pending.

I collect every little pieces of scattered trust,

My courage fragile yet firm, Figures out some hope to recover.

It yells ripping off the weave of despondency,

"Run! Chase your goals", I heard it out.

I gamble on my life again, standing over my purified hopes.

I still run for a sound sleep, a calmed mind & a nursed soul.

I still search for a sleepy night, with a dream free of hopeless solitude.

Sumit Saha

❖ The rapture had been ruptured!

I felt no compunction, only a sorrow soars

For a denying sanction what awaits at every doors.

Endeavoring wisdom bid goodbye

Straight off, incandescent died.

Zilch before my eye but a pitch-black void.

I called out the wisdom It was already home

In the quest of The Freedom, It stumbled upon The Silence's Dome.

My voice went unheard No heed, no whim

My impotent cries riverbed amidst the darkness within.

ALONE VOICE

Now look at my misery my folly cam with a cost,

I still cry over the agony of the wisdom I denied, of the light, I Lost.

Sushil Kumar

-LONELINESS:

Silence which

Had played gooseberry

For our romance,

Is now amicable to loneliness.

The day you

Hornswoggled me,

Stabbing my soul

With your treachery,

Loneliness clasped me,

Assassinating my each happiness.

Life became insipid

And legs tottered towards oblivion.

-GIRLFRIEND:

My girlfriend is so unique,

Never truants me like you.

Without resembling you,

She remains so simpatico

And renders me

Cozy lap to sleep beneath

Her raven hair.

The way she snuggles to me,

Makes me feel

That I am not alone

In this mortal world

And unlike you,

She has promised with her vivid eyes

To remain staunch to me.

Yes, she is my girlfriend,

The loneliness, which will dive into my pyre

To prove her chastity.

Swapnil Singh

-ADDICTED

No weed

No need

No merry path

In the cerebrum, I keep away from cocaine

To murder and torment, No needle in a vein

No grain to keep me rational

No sugar on a stream

No treat from desserts

ALONE VOICE

No sweet, no cheats

No stick, No liquor no juice

To pick, to utilize

No compelling reason to pardon

To interest, to confound

My medications of decision

Is none of the above?

To settle on my decision

I get high on sentimental love.

-BOO

Wearing your shirt

With your aroma on, I feel so turned on

When you are not turned on, the doorbell rings

Furthermore, I hope and run

Knowing you at an entryway.

You saw me with shirt open

Most of the way tills my waist

Inclining for you to see the view

Indeed, baby top a boo.

Tanya Gupta

-DEAR LIFE...!!

Dear life, I'm sick of you

And of the harassments that I go through.

In this world I'm left alone

And there is hardly anyone who makes me feel like own.

There is none to walk with

And happiness has become a complete myth.

Peer pressure holds a lot of irritation

And the family pressure adds up to the frustration.

I've had several sleepless nights

With wet pillows after the unwanted adjustments and fights.

Not a single soul understands me

From this egocentric world I want to flee.

In this fast running life

Even with myself I face strife.

I'm scared of losing my identity

In this world where hatred has left no amenity.

Some judge me on the behalf of my school marks,

Some on the basis of my looks give me remarks.

Though, for me they aren't at all bothered

Judgments from them I'm often offered.

I wish I'd be living in a sphere

Where I could breathe without any fear!

Vidushi Singh

 ❖ Solitary I was, flowing like a silent river in a secluded terrain.

Stormy I felt, blowing like a chilly wind over the mountains.

Silence has become my new language now, as it feels so serene and blissfully enjoyable.

Alas! You reckoned me as a lost soul, searching for peace and savor, looking to be saved.

But, darling you forgot, I'm my own savior. I don't need hero, none I want to be devoured.

I enjoy my solitude and calmness feeling exempted yet grounded from the chaos.